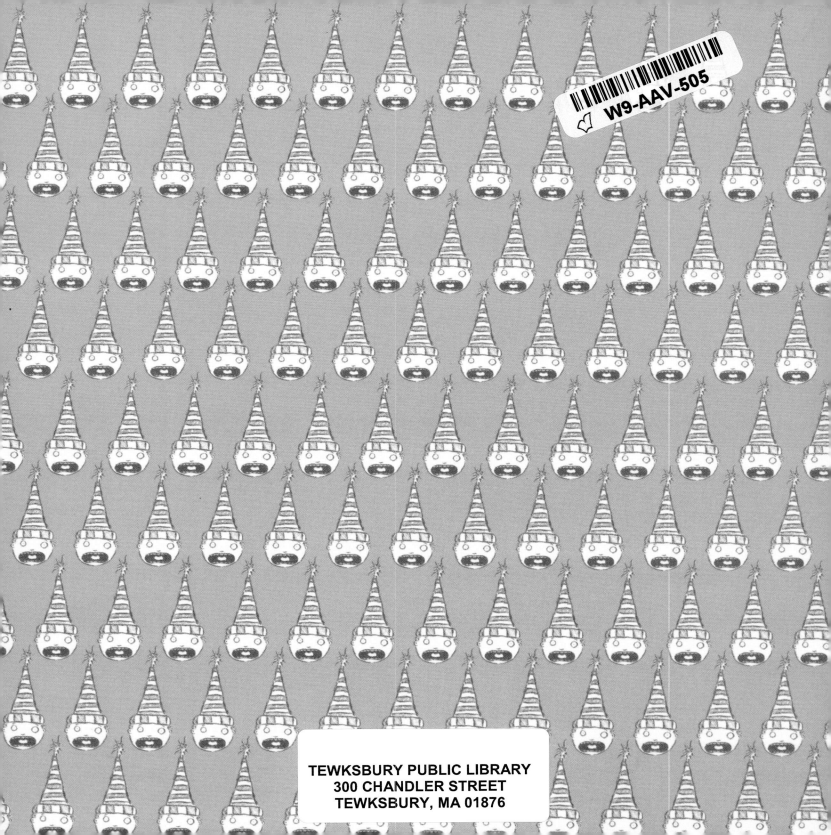

Winter Woes

Words and Pictures
by Marty Kelley

Zino Press

CHILDREN'S BOOKS
Madison, WI

Now dig this…Now dig this…
This book is for my favorite brother, Pat, who still dares
to go sledding down terrifying vertical drops with me,
even though we should both know better by now.

WINTER WOES is published by Zino Press Children's Books, PO Box 52, Madison, Wisconsin. Contents copyright © 2004 by Marty Kelley. All rights reserved. No parts of this book may be reproduced in any way, except for brief excerpts for review purposes, without the expressed written permission of Zino Press Children's Books. Printed in U.S.A.

The paintings in this book were done in watercolor on Arches paper. The text was set in Kabel.

Written and illustrated by Marty Kelley. Art direction by Patrick Ready.

Kelley, Marty.
 Winter woes / words and pictures by Marty Kelley.
     p. cm.
Summary: Rhyming lament of a young worrywart who wants to go outside and
play in the snow but fears what could happen if he does, from slipping
on steps to freezing his brain.
     ISBN 1-55933-306-5
     [1. Winter--Fiction. 2. Worry--Fiction. 3. Stories in rhyme.] I.Title.
     PZ8.3.K298Wi 2003
     [E]--dc21

                                                                                2003004717

10 9 8 7 6 5 4 3
Manufactured by Regent Publishing Services, Hong Kong,
Printed October 2009 in Shenzhen, Guangdong, China

Winter Woes

Words and Pictures
by Marty Kelley

Don't lick any frozen flagpoles!

Marty Kelley

It's snowing! It's snowing!
Hooray! Hooray!
I'll go outside
And play all day!

I'll put on my mittens
And tie my scarf tight.
I'll wear woolly socks
So I don't get frostbite.

I'll put on my hat
And my boots for the snow.
I'll put on my coat
And I'm ready to go.

But what if I put on
All of that stuff
And I get outside
And I'm not warm enough?

I might get cold,
I might get wet.
But that's not as bad
As my day could get...

What if I'm running
To go play outside
And the steps are all icy
And I slip and I slide

And I fall off the stairs
And I land on my sled
And I shoot down the hill
Heading straight for the shed

And I can't stop the sled
And the wind bites my nose
And I can't see a thing
'Cause my eyeballs are froze

And I keep going faster
And faster and faster
And I know this is going
To end in disaster

And then all at once
I slam into the shed
And an icicle falls off
And lands on my head

And I fall over backwards
And land in the snow
And I'm buried right there
For an hour or so

And I wiggle and struggle,
I'm totally trapped —
And to make matters worse
My lips get all chapped

And I finally get out
And I feel like a wreck
And ten tons of snow
Has gone right down my neck

And it's starting to melt
And it drips everywhere
And it flows like a stream
Through my long underwear

And my mittens are soggy
And they smell like old cheese
And my nose starts to run
And the boogers all freeze

And I can't wipe them off
'Cause they're frozen in place
But I try, and my mitten
Gets stuck to my face

And I can't pull it off
And I try and I try
And at last I give up
And I just start to cry

And I sob and I weep
And I bawl like a nut
And the teardrops stream down
And my eyelids freeze shut

And I can't see a thing
And I trip and I fall
And I roll down the hill
Like a giant snowball

And I tumble and bounce
And I shudder and bump
And I see that I'm speeding
Straight toward a big jump

And I surge off the jump
And up into the sky
And I keep going up
Till I'm six miles high —

And then I start falling.
I drop like a brick
And I plummet so fast
That I start to feel sick